SKOTTIE YOUNG · AARON CONLEY

IMAGE COMICS, INC.

Robert Kirkman — Chief Operating Officer
Erik Larsen — Chief Financial Officer
Todd Mcfarlane — President
Marc Silvestri — Chief Executive Officer
Jim Valentino — Vice President
Eric Stephenson — Publisher / Chief Creative Officer
Corey Hart — Director of Sales
Jeff Boison — Director of Publishing Planning & Book Trade Sales
Chris Ross — Director of Digital Sales
Jeff Stang — Director of Specialty Sales
Kat Salazar — Director of PR & Marketing
Drew Gill — Art Director
Heather Doornink — Production Director
Nicole Lapalme — Controller
IMAGECOMICS.COM

BULLY WARS, VOL. 1. First printing. February 2019. Published by Image Comics, Inc. Office of publication: 2701 NW Vaughn St., Suite 780, Portland, OR 97210. Copyright © 2019 Skottie Young & Aaron Conley. All rights reserved. Contains material originally published in single magazine form as Bully Wars #1–5. "Bully Wars," its logos, and the likenesses of all characters herein are trademarks of Skottie Young & Aaron Conley, unless otherwise noted. "Image" and the Image Comics logos are registered trademarks of Image Comics, Inc. No part of this publication may be reproduced or transmitted, in any form or by any means (except for short excerpts for journalistic or review purposes), without the express written permission of Skottie Young & Aaron Conley, or Image Comics, Inc. All names, characters, events, and locales in this publication are entirely fictional. Any resemblance to actual persons (living or dead), events, or places, without satirical intent, is coincidental. Printed in the USA. For information regarding the CPSIA on this printed material call: 203-595-3636. For international rights, contact: foreignlicensing@imagecomics.com. ISBN: 978-1-5343-1044-5.

BULLY WARS

STORY
Skottie Young

ART
Aaron Conley

COLORS
Jean-Francois Beaulieu

LETTERING
Nate Piekos of Blambot®

EDITOR
Kent Wagenschutz

DESIGN
Carey Hall

CHAPTER #1

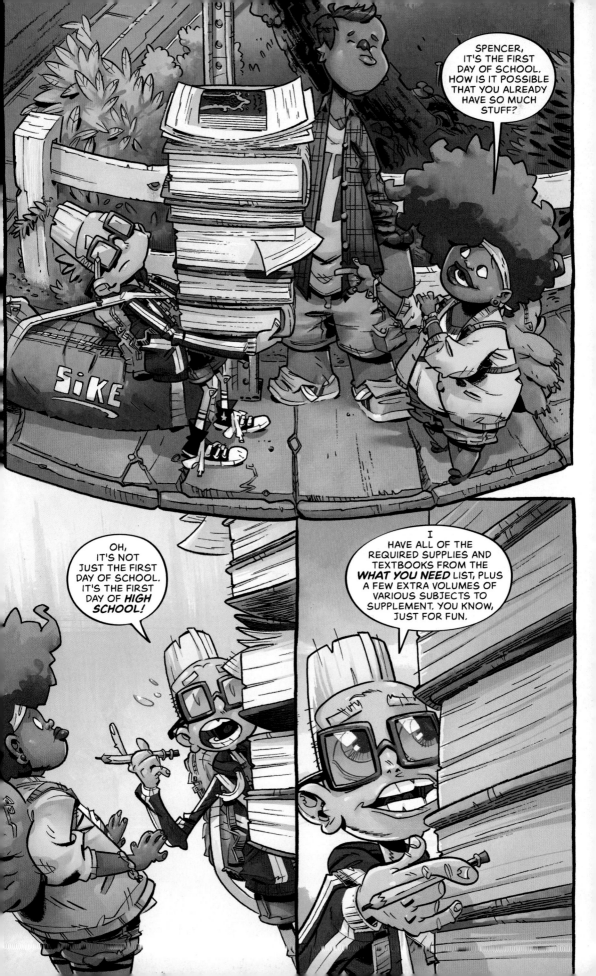

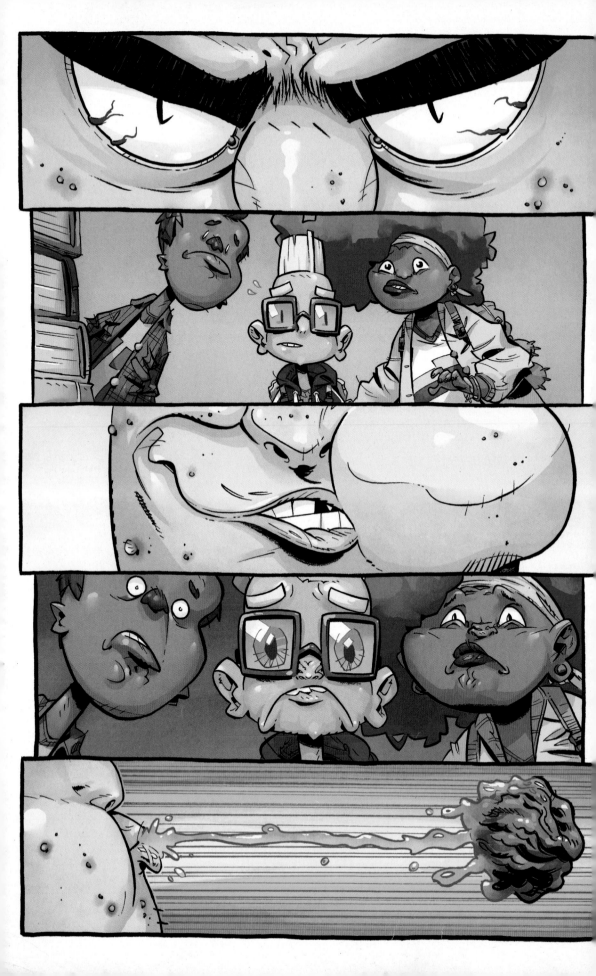

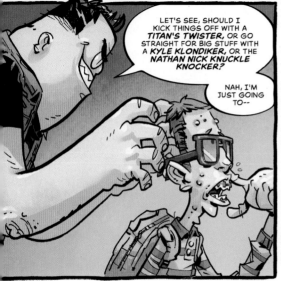

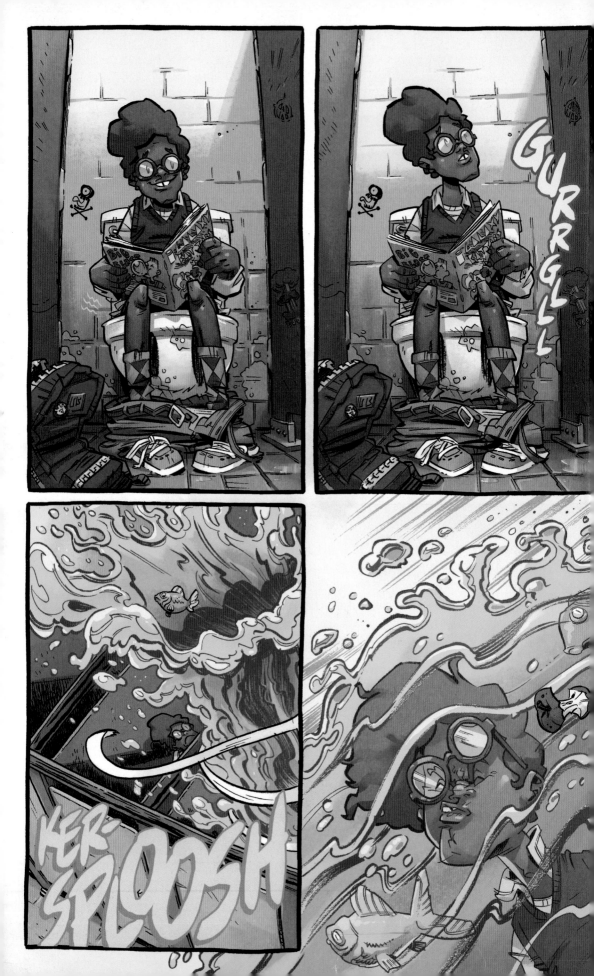

"KATIE KRUSH: SHE'S A STRAIGHT-UP BRUISER.

"IT'LL TAKE SOME PURE BRUTE STRENGTH TRAINING TO GO UP AGAINST HER.

"NICKY NEMANMEYER, GOES BY 'NOM NOM': SHE'S WORLD CHAMPION IN JUST ABOUT EVERY CATEGORY OF EATING CONTEST.

"WE'LL TRAIN YOU IN HER WAYS SO YOU CAN GET IN HER MIND.

"KARL 'CORNBREAD' KILGIS: HE SPENDS HIS DAY SHOVELING COW DUNG AND TOSSING BALES OF HAY AROUND.

"AND FINALLY, THERE'S *HOCK*. I KNOW YOU'VE HAD A FEW RUN-INS WITH HIM ALREADY, BUT HE'S MUCH, MUCH WORSE THAN YOU CAN IMAGINE--AND I KNOW YOU CAN IMAGINE SOME PRETTY DARK STUFF.

CHAPTER #3

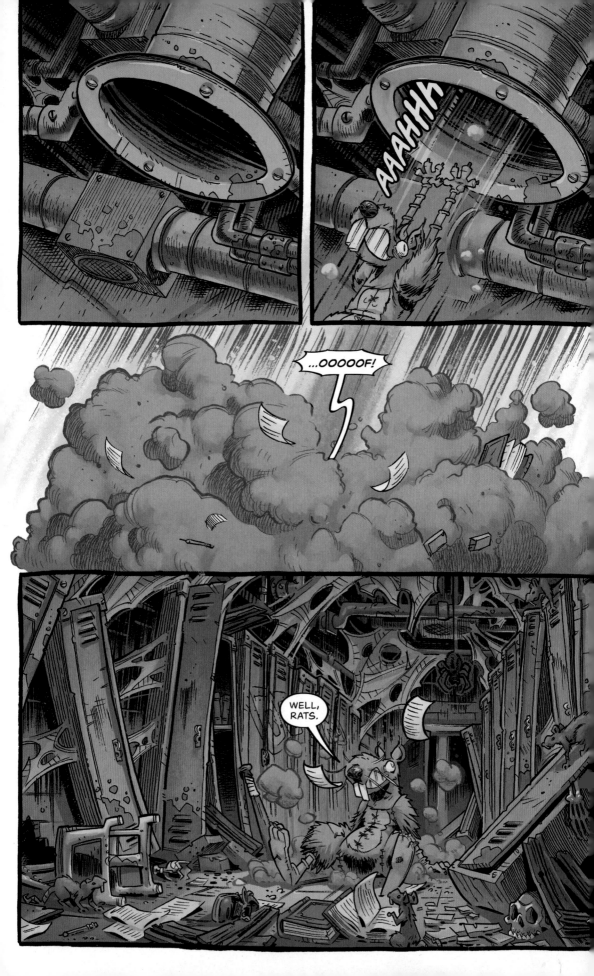

"I FIGURED I COULD PICK UP LAST WEEK'S BOOKS SINCE I WAS BUSY HELPING RUFUS TRAIN ON WEDNESDAY AND COULDN'T MAKE IT DOWN TO THE SHOP."

RIGNAROCKET REMIX
COMICS · GAMES · SMELLS

THANKS FOR DROPPING BY, SPENCER. HAVE A GOOD DAY!

...I'M IN NEED OF A *RAT!*

¡GULP!¡

THANKS, WALT! I WILL! YOU TOO!

WELL, WELL, WELL. JUST THE *NERD* I WAS LOOKING FOR...

OH, MAN. IT WAS NICE KNOWING YOU, BUDDY. I'M GONNA MISS OUR FRIEND-SHIP.

WHAT? YOU KNOW HE'S NOT DEAD, RIGHT?

HE'S TRAPPED IN THERE WITH ALL OF THOSE SAVAGES CHASING HIM. I'VE READ *LORD OF THE FLIES.* R.I.P., PIGGY.

THAT'S ALL I'M SAYING.

YOU KNOW SOMETHING IS SERIOUSLY WRONG WITH YOU, RIGHT? LIKE, YOU'RE MISSING STUFF UPSTAIRS.

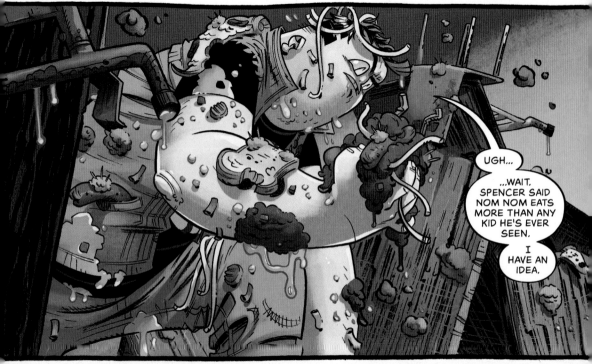

FWING

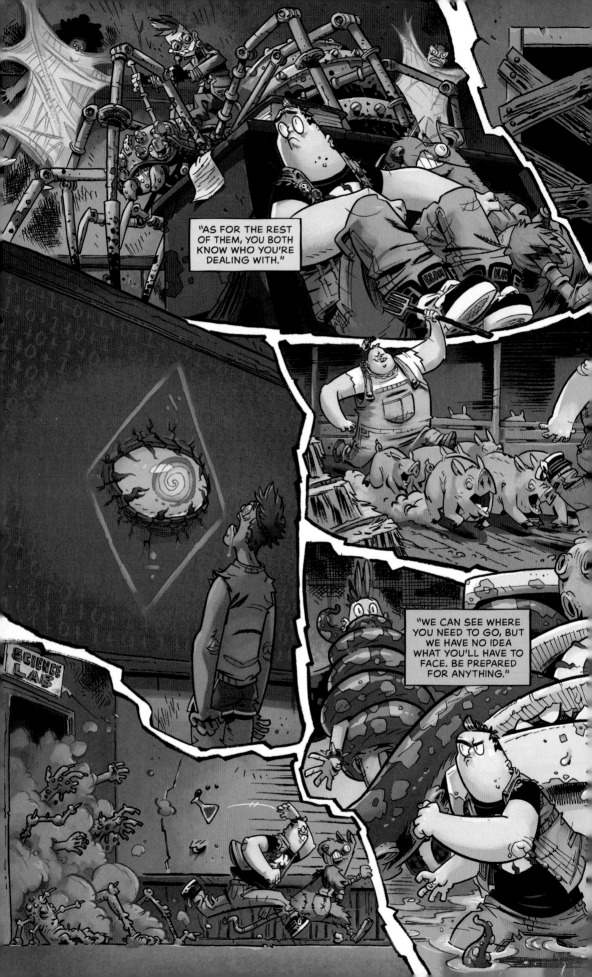

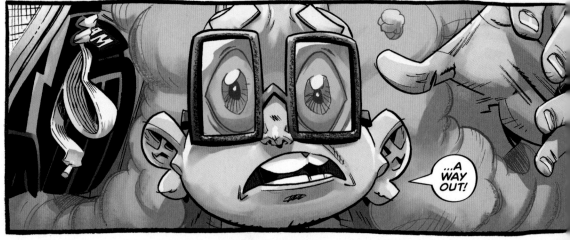

CEASE FIRE!

THE END

ISSUE ONE
COVER C
SKOTT BROWN

AARON

SKOTTIE
YOUNG
2018

ISSUE THREE
COVER B
SKOTTIE YOUNG

ISSUE FOUR
COVER B
SKOTTIE YOUNG

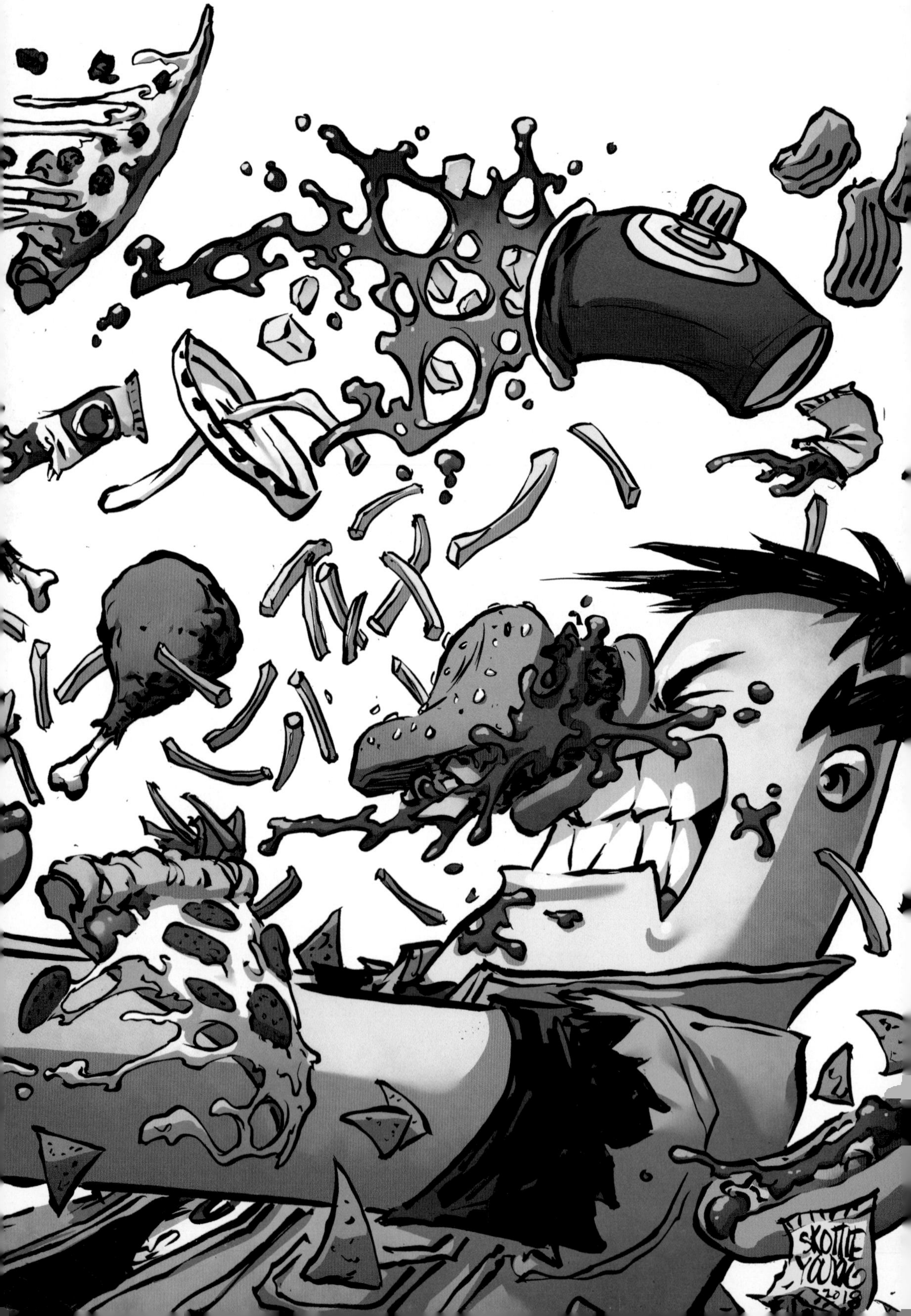

ISSUE FIVE
COVER B
SKOTTIE YOUNG

ISSUE ONE
UNUSED COVER TREATMENT
AARON CONLEY

AARON CONLEY
DEVELOPMENT SKETCHES